# Three Days in Hell

### By

### GeAnn Powers

Three Days in Hell

This book is a work of speculative fiction. While no one knows what actually happened during the three days Christ was in the tomb, this story gives one version of the events that unfolded.

# Three Days in Hell

by
GeAnn Powers

## The Day of Preparation

"Father, why do we do this?" the little boy asked.

"It is commanded by YHWH, my son. We are to do this every year to remember what he has done for us."

The boy looked at the lamb in his arms. It was a good lamb and had neither struggled nor cried when he'd picked it up. *Odd*, the lad thought.

It had been a very strange day. Gazing across the valley that morning, the boy had seen three crosses put up and a man nailed to each. The sky had darkened at midday, nearly as dark as night. When he asked his father what it was about, and the man looked over at the crosses.

"YHWH doesn't like these killings either," he said.

A few hours later, the earth had shaken. It had been violent enough to knock the lad off his feet. As he shakily rose to his feet, the sun's light returned. He looked over again at the crosses. The men on the outer crosses were still moving, trying to push themselves up on the nails through their feet. It was the only way to draw breath in that position. But the man in the middle was hanging limp. Had he died during the earthquake?

Time had marched on. Now the sun was setting low and the boy stood beside his father at the altar. Father nodded and the boy put the lamb down. The man quickly bound him with rope and the little creature lay quietly on the stones. It seemed to be waiting.

"He's a perfect little lamb," the boy said. "He doesn't have any spots or blemishes. He got to live with us in the house this week. He even slept in my bed."

"Yes, but he was chosen to pay our price."

"Tell me the story again, father."

"Ah, son! At one time, we lived in bondage. We were slaves to the Egyptians, but YHWH rescued us. That month is set as the beginning of our calendar." The father looked into his son's eyes, wanting him to know how important this was.

"Our forefathers were told," he said, "on the tenth day to look among their flocks for a lamb without spot or blemish. He was to be taken into their homes and cared for. At twilight on the fourteenth day, it's to be killed and his blood put on the doorposts. That night, death went throughout the land. Those with the blood on the doorposts were safe. But in those homes where there was no blood, the first born was taken by death and there was weeping throughout the land.

"Tomorrow is Passover," the father added. "We celebrate to remember that death passed over our people and the blood of the lamb saved us."

"And today is the day of preparation," the youth nodded. "Today, our lamb dies for us."

The father laid his hand on the quiet little animal and looked at his youngest child.

"You don't have to be here, son. You can choose to leave."

The boy looked across the valley at the three crosses. Two men were removing the body from the center one now. The sun hung very low, but the child knew neither of the other condemned men would live to see Passover.

The child reached out his hand and placed it on the lamb's head.

"I will stay, father." he said. "I want to be with him at the end."

Together, father and son watched the sun sink below the horizon.

Without speaking a word, the man raised the knife.

In another instant, the deed was done.

# Day 1

# The Underworld

"Hello, Death."

Death looked up from his desk the entrance of
Sheol and sighed. It was Lucifer. Death hadn't liked
Lucifer since he'd led them all in the Great Uprising and
the fallen angels had all ended up confined here to earth
and the underworld. Fortunately, Death was appointed as
gatekeeper to Sheol: the land of the dead. He didn't have to

see Lucifer often, but the lead fallen archangel liked to show up when a special guest arrived.

Lucifer loved to crow when an especially bad soul was escorted through the gates. The last one was Herod the Great who had groveled on the floor, trying to convince them it was all a misunderstanding. The filth covering his soul betrayed him: a blemish, sore or boil for every evil thought and deed. Herod had been so covered it was difficult to make out what his human form looked like.

Lucifer also would appear when an exceptionally good person arrived. He'd put on his show when the last great guest, John the Baptist, showed up. Unlike Herod, John barely had a mark on him. Just one or two small sins still clinging to his camel-hair tunic. Lucifer went on about how he'd had John beheaded. John's headless form just stood there, severed head tucked under his arm, grinning up at them.

Death looked over Lucifer's shoulder. From all the sores and blemishes, this guest looked like he was in the Herod category.

Well, today Lucifer was just going to have to wait. There were other souls already in the queue. Death reached out and pulled a scroll from thin air above the being standing before him. Blemished, filth: Death didn't even know what was on the scroll before he passed judgement.

"Hades," he pronounced the verdict.

"Wait! I'm a good person!" the accused stammered. "I even went to the temple three times a week!"

Death didn't have time for this song and dance story. With a loud sigh, Death motioned a demon over and gave him a nod. The demon grabbed the soul and dragged it off kicking and screaming behind him. The wall to the left opened up. Heat and smoke belched out. Death could hear the moaning and screams of those confined to that final resting place. The soul was tossed in like a filthy rag and the wall closed up again, snapping off the heat and sounds within. The dark lord shoved the scroll aside where it was caught by a second demon before it rolled off the desk. The little imp trotted off with it to be cataloged as Death dealt with the next soul.

It was the same basic story: Go to Hell. Do not pass go. Do not collect $200. Player number 2 was dragged off.

But the next one was different. Although he had spots and blemishes, when Death unrolled the scroll, something fell out that made him cringe. It was a toll pass. Literally a golden ticket. The word "Paradise" was stamped across it. Death stared at it, loathing. He'd seen millions of them through the years, and like a million times before, he reached for it. No dice. Just like all the times before he couldn't touch it. A force field held it to the table for everyone to see.

Death growled.

"Take it," he snarled, glaring down at the soul.

Timidly, a hand shakily reached out, and the ticket didn't resist. The recipient's eyes widened in wonder at the precious gift.

"Over there." Death jerked his head to the right, indicating where the soul should go. Hesitantly, the man obeyed. As he came to the wall of the cavern, it melted away and before him was a great gulf. On the other side, one could see an endless green field with trees and flowers and other beings laughing and playing. The man stared in awe. A bridge materialized in front of his feet, spanning the wide gap. The soul just stood there, unsure what to do.

"GO!" Death roared.

That got him moving. The man was to the other side in moments. The bridge faded, and the wall reappeared, erasing any hint of what had just happened.

Death shook his head, disgusted. Just like John the headless Baptist. Grumbling, he turned to the next being in line, grabbed the scroll and ripped it open.

"Hades," he announced.

"But what about…" the man wondered, pointing at the wall where the bridge had been moments before.

"HADES!"

A demon clamped a hand around the soul and towed him off.

Another soul shuffled forward, covered in filthy rags. Lucifer grabbed the scroll and unfurled it. Another ticket dropped out. Another ticket to paradise. Death stared hard at the man and then down at the scroll.

"Says here you're a thief," Death remarked.

The man nodded. "Yes," he meekly admitted. "But I was promised I'd be in paradise before nightfall."

Death growled so savagely, the soul shrank back a few steps.

"Take it!" Death spat.

The ticket was hastily snatched, the bridge appeared, and the wall was back in seconds. Death dropped the scroll on the desk, and it rolled back up on itself. A little demon waited there expectantly, but Death didn't brush the scroll his way. Instead, he left it lying there. The dark lord wanted to look deeper into this. He was used to clean spirits getting tickets, but that filthy pick-pocket?

Three more souls had been dragged away to the left before Lucifer stepped up to the desk. Death sighed loudly. He really wasn't in the mood for this.

"What ya got today, Lu?" Death asked the host.

The lord of darkness frowned. "I told you not to call me that," he reminded Death and quickly looked around to see if the other demons had heard. No one seemed to notice. They were all warily looking over Lucifer's guest, being careful not to get too close.

Death glared down at Lucifer with a scowl to remind the dark lord that, ruler of Hades or not, Death was not someone he wanted to reckon with. "What ya got today, Lu?"

Lucifer decided to ignore the transgression.

"I got him, Death!" he cackled gleefully. "I finally got him! It's him! The big guy! The Big G! He made himself human, and we killed him! He's ours now!" Lucifer turned with a huge grin and grandly gestured to the latest soul to enter Sheol's foyer.

Death frowned. What was Lucifer talking about? This fellow was even more encrusted with blemishes and filth than Herod. He could hardly stand from all the sin that clung to him. The wretched being had hobbled his way in, leaving bloody footprints in his wake. He certainly didn't look like any god. But then again… Death hesitated. There was something off about this soul.

Even Lucifer blinked. "He didn't look that bad when I first got him," he admitted with a cackle, "but I gotta say, the change is an improvement! We took the long way getting here. I guess he must have picked up some stains on the way."

Death shook his head, trying to make sense of this. "This is The Almighty? But God's immortal."

"The idiot made himself into a human! A normal human! He was born in that gross human way, grew up, had zits, got hairy, the whole kit and caboodle! He's really human! Or, he WAS. We killed him a few hours ago. Crucified! Oh, it was glorious to watch!" Lucifer chortled at the memory, still fresh in his mind.

Okay, Death had to admit, that was pretty impressive. Not the worst demise he'd ever heard of, but definitely in the top five. He personally liked it when the victims were staked down and eaten alive by fire ants, but a crucifixion was always good, too. He glanced over at the prisoner again and gasped.

"Is he getting bigger?"

"What?" Lucifer looked too. "Well, what do you know? He is! He has even more sin on him now than before! They're five deep in places!" Lucifer hooted with laughter. "I never imagined killing him would have this effect!"

Death stared, agog, trying to figure out what was happening. He saw movement on the floor and pointed.

"Where in heaven did THAT come from?"

"No need to swear!" Lucifer abashed him, but he looked too. There on the floor, a single small sin wiggling its way across the chamber. When it got to the prisoner, it crawled up his leg and was absorbed into the rest of the muck and filth. As they watched, Death noticed another sin likewise making its way across the cavern. Another came out of a crack in the wall, escaping from a prisoner's cell on the other side.

Death turned his head and noticed other sins making their way to the prisoner. Within moments, more were coming to join them.

"Why, look!" Lucifer said. "I think they all want a piece of him! Know what this means, Death? We've won this time! We've really done it!"

Death wasn't so sure. Nothing like this had ever happened before and none of it made sense. More and more sins were coming, all drawn to the new arrival. Faster and faster they traveled, frantic to get there. As if they were being called…

Death came out from behind his desk and cautiously approached this God / man. He reached into the air above his head and pulled out … nothing. Death tried again and still came up empty. He waved his hand in the air, searching, but there was nothing there. No scroll. No death contract.

Death whirled on Lucifer.

"What was his crime?" he demanded.

Lucifer blinked. "What?"

"There's no death contract! What did he do?"

"Well," Lucifer scratched his head. "Nothing," he admitted. "He'd never sinned at all."

"That's not possible!" Death argued. "They ALL sin!"

One of the little demons standing on the sidelines dared to creep forward. He scuttled over to one of the bloody footprints and began lapping at the liquid. After only a few licks though, he screamed in pain.

"It burns! It burns!" he shrieked.

Another demon came and stuck a finger in the blood. He felt the smudge, rolling his thumb over the red substance, and shook his head.

"It doesn't feel right," he hissed.

Death turned to Lucifer again, panic in his voice.

"Who are his parents? You said he was born, so he had human parents, right?"

"Yeah, his mom is this girl named Mary…"

"And the father?" Death prompted. "Who was the father?"

Lucifer wasn't smiling now.

"WHO?" Death barked. "The death curse is passed down through Adam. He would have inherited it from his father. WHO WAS HE?"

Lucifer still said nothing. Instead, he raised a hand, uncurling a finger, and pointed up.

Death flinched back in horror. "Lu! You fool!" he spat.

"I told you not to call me that!" the devil hissed.

"You're an idiot!" Death snapped. "You killed an innocent man!"

"Who cares? Just shove him in with the holier-than-thou group."

But He's sinless, and you killed him!"

"So, what's the big deal?"

"Death is a punishment, you buffoon! It's the punishment for sin, but he's never sinned! He's never committed a sin, he wasn't even born in sin. You killed him for something he never committed! You broke the rules! And he's GOD!"

Lucifer glowered. "Okay, I'll put him back. He can be alive again."

Death threw up his hands. "You can't just 'put him back'! You broke the contract! It has to be repaid for full value!"

"I said I'd put him back!" Lucifer shouted back.

Death glared at him. When he spoke again, his voice was very low.

"Just what's the value of a god's life, Lu?" he queried. "Especially if it has a big G?"

It took a moment for the full meaning of that question to sink in, and Lucifer's eyes got very big.

The two dark lords stared at each other. They shifted their gaze to their guest. The blob of sin was immense now and a few last remnants hurriedly slithered across the floor to join the others.

"That's a lot of bad," Death whispered, awed by the enormity.

"I think he absorbed it all," Lucifer whispered back, finally realizing what was going on.

"What? Why?"

Lucifer offered the only viable explanation. "Because he can."

Something was happening. The darkened blob was starting to smoke. Red, molten cracks appeared on the surface. As they widened, white light flooded out in beams, blinding the inhabitants of the chamber. The little demons screamed and ran in terror. Lucifer and Death stood there, frozen in their places. The fissures widened until the sin could no longer contain what was within. With a mighty boom, it shattered, sending shock waves out before it, so strong they shook the foundations of Sheol and knocked Lucifer and Death to the ground. The shards of sin, consumed in the white light, fluttered to the floor as ash.

The two dark lords looked up from their place on the floor. There, standing where the crippled, blemished guest had been, was the mighty Lord of Lords, pure white light radiating from him.

Lucifer and Death slowly rose to their feet, terrified. A demon ran up and cowered behind the dark lords, putting them between itself and the Lord.

"You're majesties! It's the prisoners!"

Death and Lucifer whirled around. "What about the prisoners?" they demanded.

The little demon swallowed hard. "The humans in Paradise are all spotless and glowing! Like HIM!" He pointed at Jesus, horrified.

"Great," Death muttered under his breath. "He's contagious."

"And some of them escaped!" the demon continued. "Just a handful, but they've gone back up to the human world!"

"Just like a few months ago when Lazarus slipped out of our clutches," Death hissed in Lucifer's ear.

The voices had drawn Jesus' attention. He turned to them with blazing eyes.

He spoke a single word: "Tetelestai!"

"*It is Finished.*" Death translated, though it wasn't necessary, for Lucifer knew Greek as well. Confused, Death turned to the dark archangel. "What's he talking about? What's finished?"

A nasty pit opened up in Lucifer's gut. He could feel his insides churning like a lava pit.

*What have I done?* he wondered.

# The Over World

"Edem! Edem!"

Edem came out of her house as the man ran up to the gate. He stopped, panting and out of breath.

"Gideon!" Edem scowled. "It's the Passover! No running allowed today! Or tomorrow either. That's the Unleavened Bread Sabbath. And the day after that is Shabbot. You'll have to wait until the day after that for your foolishness."

The man shook his head. "I saw him!" he gasped. "I saw Joash!"

Edem frowned. "Don't tease me, Gideon. My husband has been dead for three weeks now. How dare you disrespect his name."

The man vehemently protested. "No Edem!" he insisted. "He's alive! I saw him! The earthquake yesterday: it opened some of the graves in the cemetery. Joash came out of his grave and headed to Jerusalem! Come: I'll take you!"

The man took the woman's hand and half dragged her behind him. Shocked, Edem hurried along trying not to be pulled over. This behavior was totally inexcusable. What if her neighbors saw? She quickly glanced around. The hills were crowded with tents and ramshackle huts that had popped up with the huge throngs that had flooded into the countryside around the city. The streets were packed with people from all over the known world. Passover was a huge celebration, and thousands were there to see Herod's amazing temple he'd built to the Jewish God. Gideon weaved his way through them, forcing Edem to follow. Across the bridge and into the temple mount complex they pushed, trying to get to the front of the crowd.

The court of the gentiles was packed with spectators, all murmuring, wondering at everything they'd seen and heard the day before.

"Did you hear about Jesus?" someone asked, but Edem and Gideon were past them before Edem could hear the rest.

"Caiaphas tore his robe at Jesus' trial," another said. "Wouldn't that disqualify him as high priest?"

"Yeah, but only until he changed his clothes," a voice answered as Edem was dragged by them.

"The sky turned black! At mid-day!" Edem caught from another conversation they whizzed past.

"Did you see the curtain in the temple? It's been destroyed! Torn in half!"

"And that earthquake! It knocked over Joshua Ben Simon's house! They were lucky to get out alive!"

Edem tried to stop. She knew Joshua and his family and she wanted to ask about them, but Gideon rushed her on. They pushed onward and into the Court of Woman. Edem tried to wrestle her hand away. This was as far as she was allowed to go, but Gideon ignored her protest. She was pulled farther in, and into the Men's courtyard. Edem's cheeks turned red with shame. She would be expelled, maybe even barred from ever entering the temple area again for this. But no one seemed to notice. Everyone was staring at the steps in front of the temple. Edem raised her eyes to see what was going on. A group of about a dozen people were gathered there, but Edem had never seen people like this. Their robes were whiter than snow and they were glowing. Everyone was standing back from these strangers, but no one could look away from the spectacle. They were speaking, shouting, so all could hear them.

"It's been done!" they proclaimed. "The Messiah has come! He paid the price for us! Death is conquered!"

As Edem stared, a tall man in their midst turned around.

"Joash!" She shrieked, instantly recognizing her late husband.

The man blinked and looked at her. A small smile spread across his lips.

"Joash!" Edem cried again. She ran up to the temple steps, not caring who saw her there now, and reached out for him. But Joash put up his hands and backed away.

"Don't touch me!" he commanded. "We are the first fruits! If you touch us, we will be tainted! We have come to present ourselves to the high priest before we go to YHWH. We are here to tell of the fulfilled prophecies!"

"Caiaphas! Caiaphas!" the people around the murmured. Where was Caiaphas the high priest? He was quickly summoned and hurried to the temple steps. When he saw the white robed figures, he stopped and stared, stunned.

Joash smiled at him. "We are the first fruits," he repeated. "We have come from Paradise and have been sent on ahead by the Messiah. He will be returning in a few days."

Caiaphas blinked, uncomprehending. "The Messiah?"

"Yes! Jesus whom you crucified! He is the Christ - the Chosen one. He came and released us to go on ahead. We are the first fruits and were sent to present ourselves to the high priest and tell him of what has happened!"

Caiaphas' eyes nearly bulged out of his head. "Jesus was the devil! He is dead and rotting in Hades! Who are you? How dare you speak to me like that! I shall have you thrown out!"

Joash's smile faded and he stared hard at Caiaphas. Finally, he shook his head. "You are the high priest, but you are not *our* high priest," he said. "His blood has been spilled. The final sacrifice has been made; the price has been paid. It is finished. Salvation has come to earth. The way is now open to the Mercy Seat of God."

Joash turned with a wave, inviting all to look. Edem craned her neck to see. The doors to the temple stood open. Eden looked through the doors and into the temple, past the golden lampstand and incense burner to the back room: the Holy of Holies. The place where the Ark of the Covenant had stood in Solomon's day. The Mercy Seat of God. No one could enter the Holy of Holies except the high priest, and only once a year. On that day, the priest would pour blood on the Mercy Seat to symbolically cover the sins of the people. The Holy of Holies was cordoned off from the rest of the temple by a huge veil, sixty feet tall, thirty feet wide and four inches thick. But not today. The veil - that incredibly thick tapestry - hung tattered, torn in two, from top to bottom.

"Your salvation is no longer found here!" Joash told the crowd. "Salvation is only found through the true sacrifice that was made by Jesus, the Messiah! He's paid the price for our sins with his own blood when he died on a cross!"

"Enough!" Caiaphas shouted. "Guards! Seize them!"

The temple guards rushed forward, but Joash and the others disappeared from sight, leaving only the stunned masses behind.

Edem stared at the spot her dead husband had been only moments before. Her gaze shifted up to the torn curtain.

*What does this mean?* She wondered. *What does it mean?*


Caiaphas licked his dry lips, shaken. What had this man meant, speaking of Jesus like that? Caiaphas had Jesus killed just yesterday, nailed to a cross by the Romans. Why was this man claiming Jesus was the Messiah?

The high priest looked around. Not far away was the captain of the temple guards, staring at him, wondering what to do. Caiaphas motioned him over.

"Aren't there guards posted at Jesus' tomb?" he asked in a low voice.

"Yes, Rabbi. Pilate ordered them there himself."

"The tomb has not been disturbed in any way?"

"No, Rabbi. I would have been sent word. Nothing is amiss."

Caiaphas nodded. "See if you can get the guard doubled," he suggested. "Jesus' disciples might seize upon this lunacy to try stealing the body and claim he's come back to life."

The guard nodded. "Right away, Rabbi," he promised, and turned away to see that Caiaphas' request was carried out. Meanwhile, the high priest pondered what the man in white had said to him:

*Jesus was the Messiah, the Christ.*

Well, Jesus was dead, so that was a lie.

*Joash and the others had been sent on ahead as first fruits.* First Fruits was the offering to God from the first of the harvest. Harvest of what? People weren't harvested!

*Jesus would be returning in a few days.*

Caiaphas felt his heart skip a beat. Jesus returning? No…he couldn't…. He couldn't be the Messiah…

But Caiaphas closed up his heart and mind, refusing to even let the thought complete itself. Jesus was dead, and that was that. Joash was a lunatic, prematurely buried and had somehow escaped his tomb. Now the man was spreading lies. The shiny robes must have been just bleach. The matter was closed.

Still, the thought persisted in nagging him.

*But what if? What if?*

## Day 2

## The Feast of Unleavened Bread

"Mother, why do we eat this flat bread?" the little girl asked.

"It's to remember our forefathers as they came out of Egypt," she replied. "The morning after death passed through Egypt, Pharoah finally let our people go. They left so quickly they didn't have time to let their bread rise. On their way to the Red Sea, they ate flat bread like this. It took them a week to get there. But they didn't know Pharoah was following them with his armies. At the sea, Pharoah though the Israelites were caught, but YHWH parted the sea for them to cross to the other side. When Pharoah's men tried to cross, the sea closed up and devoured them. Now on the other side, YHWH gave our people manna to eat until they came to the promised land."

"So, we can't eat anything with leaven in it for seven days?"

"No, my little one. I have cleared out all the leaven jars and swept the house clean. Not one speck of leaven is there to be found."

"But why mother? Why can't we have any leaven?"

"Daughter, what happens when a little leaven is put into the dough?"

"It puffs up."

"All of it, or just part?"

"Why, all of it, of course!"

"That is how sin is, child. A little sin can corrupt the whole body. So, we cleaned out all the leaven to symbolically remove sin from our house. YHWH wants us to be pure and sinless. Yesterday was Passover, and a lamb was slaughtered to cover us from death. He paid our price. I think we can give up leaven for a few days, don't you?"

The little girl thought very hard. She liked leavened bread best, but should she be so selfish when the lamb had given its life for them? After all, it was only for a week.

"Yes, mother," she answered. "I can give it up."

# The Underworld

"What's he doing now?" Lucifer wanted to know.

Death scowled. This was all Lucifer's fault. Death didn't even bother to answer.

The place was a shambles. Jesus had never said another word to Death or Lucifer. He'd only turned his attention to the cavern wall behind them, and it crumbled and collapsed under his gaze, exposing the gulf beyond it. On the other side was Paradise. The people there were looking expectantly over to them, their eyes focus on Jesus. Behind them, there was a huge crack. Some of them had left through there, but most remained, choosing to quietly wait.

There was no bridge. Instead, Jesus simple walked across on the air. He was over there, talking to the clean ones now.

Death had no time for this. The foyer was filling up with souls, many of them there because of the earthquake that had happened just minutes before. They stared at the scene around them. Death was used to souls arriving, often in a state of terror, but this wasn't terror now. It was bewilderment. He whirled around, glaring at Lucifer.

"What now, Genius?" he demanded.

"He's going to take them out," one of the little demons speculated. "He's going to take them through that crack and lead them out of here."

"Where?" Lucifer snapped. "They're not allowed to leave: it's in the contracts! They'll all sinners, even if they're cleaner than most. They're stuck here with the rest!"

"But…" the demon swallowed hard, hesitant to answer. "They're all clean like him! There's not a spot on any of them!"

"They can't leave!" Lucifer insisted. "The contracts are binding!"

Death sighed loudly. "Why do I have a feeling we are about to find out otherwise?" he grimaced.

Lucifer glared at him. "It's the law!" he insisted. "It's the death law! They have to pay the penalty! They all have contracts!"

"Then how were those others able to leave?" Death wanted to know.

Lucifer huffed so hard, fire shot out of his nose. The little demon was standing a bit too close and yelped. The Under Lords ignored him.

"We'll see the bookkeeper about this!" Lucifer announced. "He'll show you I'm right."

Death nodded agreement. He snatched the thief's contract off his desk and stuffed it into his pocket. Then, the two dark angels strolled off together, leaving the little demon frantically hopping around to cool off his singed bottom.

The bookkeeper wasn't too happy to see the two rulers in his domain. He looked up from his precious scrolls and documents, glaring.

"We need to see the contracts on the souls in Paradise," Lucifer demanded. He glared back at the other, daring him to oppose him. The bookkeeper worked his jaw, red eyes locked on Lucifer's as he slowly rose from his desk. He would follow orders, but he wasn't going to break any speed records doing it. He walked through his chambers, scanning the innumerable pigeonholes in his domain, pulling out one scroll after another. When he had an armful, he slowly lurched back to the desk and dropped them there.

Lucifer grabbed one, broke the seal and unrolled it. Death, looking over his shoulder, gasped in surprise.

"The marks!" he stammered. "I saw them there just a second ago! They'll all gone!"

Puzzled, the bookkeeper craned his neck to get a look at the parchment. It was as clear as the day it was made.

"That isn't possible…" The bookkeeper took up a different scroll, ripped through the seal with his taloned fingernail and unrolled it. For a split second, he saw the marks in their proper places. But as soon as the scroll was open to the foul air, it was wiped clean.

The bookkeeper blinked, uncomprehending. What was going on?

"The thief's contract…" Death quickly drew it out of his pocket, but the writing on it disappeared before their eyes.

The three Under Lords grabbed up scroll after scroll tearing them open with the same results for each. The bookkeeper could feel the cold sweat trickling down his back.

"Inconceivable!" he murmured "How…what…???"

Lucifer came to a dead stop, a horrified look on his face.

"What about…" he croaked out, "the Aggregate Scroll?"

Death and the bookkeeper stared at him. Dread entered their eyes as they suddenly caught the same thought as Lucifer.

With trembling hands, the bookkeeper took down the huge, thick scroll from its sacred holder on the wall. He looked up at the others, all terrified by what they might find. He laid the scroll down on the table and slowly began unrolling it.

The Aggregate Scroll: the record of all history with every person ever born from the time of creation, and all their sins recorded. As it unrolled, they watched in agony as marks began disappearing. Abel, Eve, Adam, Seth…not every mark was wiped away, but a significant amount were. Lucifer recognized each one. They were the sins of these now sitting in Paradise. Each sin of theirs was being erased. Every single sin.

"But…but…" the bookkeeper stammered, "they all had contracts. They were all sinners…"

"The contacts were all nullified and paid for," Death growled, glaring at Lucifer.

"What?" the bookkeeper blinked, trying to understand. "How?"

"He killed God's son," Death spat out, pointing a gnarled finger at Lucifer. "The Almighty took on human form, but he never sinned. Lucifer killed him anyway. He broke the rules. That contract has to be paid back in full."

"Full?!?" the bookkeeper's eyes bugged out so far, they nearly fell out. "But that's impossible! That cost would be infinite!"

Death waved at the disappearing marks on the scroll. "So, I guess he's taking it in change," he commented, sarcastically.

Lucifer was bent over the parchment. He'd unrolled it past the flood, the Egyptian and Babylonian empires, the Maccabean wars, and to that very day's accounting.

"WHAT?" he shrieked. "That isn't fair! He's wiping out the records of people who haven't even died yet!"

"Well," Death shrugged, "He's God, so…" He shook his head, disgusted.

"What's this mean?" Lucifer demanded, jabbing a pointing finger at one entry. "It was solid black. It's now grey. What's that mean?"

Death and the bookkeeper stared, trying to make sense of it. There were more marks fading to grey also. Thousands more. The bookkeeper had no answer. Nothing like this had ever happened before on his watch.

"Potential," Death finally guessed. "Not washed away yet, but could be at some future time. That's my theory anyway." He squinted down at the tiny name beside one mark that had just gone grey. "Saul of Tarsus. Better keep an eye on that one, Lu." Death quipped, clapping Lucifer on the shoulder.

Lucifer didn't bother to respond as he stared down at the sea of sin, more and more fading to grey by the second. Hundreds, thousands, millions.

A breeze ruffled the parchment. A cool breeze.

*What the…?*

The breeze picked up and grew into a wind, whipping through the corridors, pushing out the foul stench of decay before it. Lucifer spun around to locate the source of the rushing gale. Coming from across the gulf was a light, and it was growing brighter and stronger.

A cold sweat broke out on Lucifer's face and a shiver ran down his spine.

It was a cold day in Hell, indeed.

# Day 2

## The Upper World

"Joash?"

The old man stopped his preaching and turned around.

"Nicodemus!" Joash was glad to see his friend. "What are you doing here?"

"I…I heard you were back from the dead and came to see for myself."

Joash looked down at himself as if just realizing his risen body and smiled. "Yes," he admitted. "I guess I am back. For now. I will be leaving soon, though. Do not touch me, my friend. We are the first fruits and must remain untainted."

The first fruits? Nicodemus shook his head, not comprehending. The Festival of First Fruits was coming soon, he knew, but what did this have to do with the first harvest festival? Nicodemus would try to figure that out later. There were so many questions he had.

"Joash, what happened?" he wanted to know.

"Well," Joash gathered his thoughts. "I died. I died and went to Paradise." He got a far off, dreamy look in his eye as he recalled the experience. "So many people were there, Nicodemus. I saw my mother and father, of course, but so many others too! Good King David was there, and Samuel the prophet. And Noah, and so many others. It was beautiful there, and we were happy, but we were all waiting."

"Waiting for what?"

"To be with YHWH, of course! We all knew of him, and we all longed to see him, but we had to wait."

"But why?" Nicodemus wanted to know. "You'd honored YHWH all your life! Why weren't you taken to heaven?"

Joash shook his head sadly. "Because we were all tainted. We couldn't go into YHWH's presence that way. Even the good prophet Moses was there! We were all waiting for the day we could finally see him face to face.

Adam could remember him, and he often cried in longing. So, we were happy to be there, but very sad too.

"And then, it happened." Joash said. "There was a great earthquake that shook Paradise. A large crack appeared, and a voice told me to go. Those of us here all heard it and we all came back up to here. I was back in the tomb, but the slab had been broken so I could come out. Look, my friend! This is me! My body! But my soul has been washed clean! It was the messiah, Nicodemus! We saw him! He paid with his life so we are pure and can go to YHWH now! But first, he wanted us to come back here and tell others. It was Jesus! He died and he's coming back!"

"But Joash, Caiaphas is looking for you. The temple guard has instructions to hunt you down and kill you and everyone with you. They are headed here now!"

Joash smiled and shook his head. "Don't worry, my friend. They cannot hurt us. I already died once, remember? What more can they do to me? We stand between the worlds, Nicodemus. We are between the world of the living and the world of YHWH. We can see his angels on the hillsides. He is looking out for us.

"Oh, my friend!" Joash continued, looking past his companion. "It is so beautiful! It's brighter than you can imagine! There is perfect peace in the other world! I can see the hosts of heaven and the cherubim at the gates of heaven! The gates are ready to open, Nicodemus! I see, I see…"

"What?" Nicodemus implored. "What is it, Joash?"

Joash stared; his eyes focused beyond what the other could see.

"What is it?" Nicodemus begged. "What do you see, Joash?"

A small smile came to Joash's face, and tears glistened in his eyes as he gazed in awe and wonder.

"Everything!"

# Day 3

## Shabbot

## (The Saturday Sabbath Day)

"Eliazer Ben Simon! What do you think you are doing?"

The teen had been chasing his younger siblings around the yard, but he came to a screeching halt at the stern sound of his mother's voice.

"Nothing, Ema," he replied.

"There is no running on the Sabbath!" his mother scolded. "It's bad enough I have to remind your brother and sister, but you are old enough to know the laws! Even YHWH rested on the Sabbath. And our forefathers were not even allowed to gather manna on that day; they had to gather twice as much the day before so they could keep the Sabbath holy."

Eliazer sighed noisily. "But Ema," he whined. "Did you not hear what the prophet Jesus said when we listened to him preach? Man was not made for the Sabbath: the Sabbath was made for Man! Jesus healed people on the Sabbath. He even let his disciples gather grain in the fields on that day. I don't think he would be upset by children laughing and playing on a day YHWH has blessed."

"Jesus is dead," his mother reminded him. "I doubt that he's doing anything at all today."

# The Underworld

"*Now* what's he doing?" Lucifer asked, his voice high and screechy. Death glared at him.

*If you can't keep from sounding like a little girl, keep your mouth shut!* he silently scolded. They stood there in the foyer, he and bookkeeper, as Lucifer paced the rapidly shrinking floor space. More souls had poured in, but Death had no interest in processing them at that moment. The humans cowered against the wall trying to stay away from the dark lords. The poor souls stared around, trying to make sense of what was going on.

One of the little demons ran up to give a report. "He's going through every level of Sheol," he said. "All the locks are melting just with his touch. He's talking to the prisoners and rounding up the guards."

"Why?" Lucifer wanted to know.

"He's saying things. Horrible things!" the small imp was terrified. "He's finding us and telling us what will happen when…when…"

"When what?" the dark lord commanded.

The answer came out in a tiny, shaking voice. "When he takes over." The creature shook his head. "It's going to be even worse than before. It's going to be the end for us."

Death blinked, stunned. "He's not taking over *now*?"

"I don't think so. He kept saying 'next time'. 'Next time'. My lord, he's planning another battle. A big one. One that will determine who really rules the earth for once and for all." The demon pointed to the other side of the abyss to Paradise. "That's his army, he says. Them and the others on earth who follow him. But they aren't going to be doing the fighting. Just him. Just that one they call Jesus."

All the demons stared at this evil little prophet, thunderstruck. After a few moments, quiet murmuring broke out.

"He cast all of us into a herd of pigs when he was a human," the demons of Legion had whispered to some of the others. "He's even more powerful now."

"He could control the sea and the wind," another nodded. "He's more powerful than the Dark Lord."

Lucifer overheard that and turned on his minions. With a wave of his hand, they were all left writhing on the floor in agony.

Death straightened up and nudged the bookkeeper. "He's coming back."

The bookkeeper looked in the direction Death was staring. There was that light, coming from the depths of Hades and getting brighter. The two stood up and moved back out of the way. Lucifer noticed and turned to see the light also. He stood his ground though.

In a few minutes, the Lord of Lords was there in their midst. He walked right past, headed for Paradise. The bookkeeper perked up at that and licked his lips.

"Uh…they all have contracts…" he began.

Jesus raised one hand. The millions of now-blank contracts flew from the bookkeeper's domain, heeding the call. To their Lord they flew, but none reached him. Once in his precense, they dissolve into dust.

One of the human souls pressed against the wall stared at Jesus face.

"I know you!" he yelped. "You healed me of leprosy!"

Jesus stopped in his tracks and turned. Spotting the man, he smiled and held out a hand. The man, one of the cleaner souls, ran to him and flung himself into Jesus' arms.

"Thank you, thank you, thank you!" the man wept, his head buried in Jesus' shoulder.

"It's Jesus! It's the Messiah!" Others came forward and touched their Lord, awed. All of them turned white as snow.

Seeing what happened, another in the crowd pushed his way forward.

"Me, Jesus, take me too!" he demanded. "I'm a good person. I was in the synagogue every sabbath! Don't leave me here with these sinners!"

Jesus stared at him. "You never knew me," he told the man.

"I just as good as those others, Lord!" the soul insisted. "I don't belong here. This place is for evil people. Like THEM!" He pointed to the others, cowered on the wall. Most didn't even dare look at Jesus. And all were covered with blemishes. Just like the soul now shouting his innocence.

Jesus took the hand of the leper but left the other behind.

They turned toward the wall, and it dissolved, exposing the great gulf before them. The bridge appeared for the final time.

"NO!" Lucifer shrieked. "You can't take them! I won't let you!"

He flung himself at the Lord but was thrown back and sprawled on the floor. Instantly, Jesus was standing over him, his foot on Lucifer's head, crushing down on it. Lucifer writhed against the pain. It only lasted a moment, then stopped. But the foot remained.

"I created you," Jesus reminded him. "It doesn't end here. We will meet again, and you will meet your doom."

The foot was removed. Jesus glanced over at Death and the bookkeeper. Neither would meet his gaze.

"I'll see you again too," Jesus reminded them, "and the three of you will be dealt with. Your futures, like your pasts are entangled for eternity. And for all eternity, you will be reminded of that." His gaze took in Lucifer, Death, the bookkeeper, and the other dark demons gathered listening. It wasn't a warning. It was a proclamation.

Some trembled. Some looked away. Some glared back in defiance. All understood the Lord's meaning.

Jesus turned back again to the bridge, ready to lead the others across.

"Where are we going?" a small voice asked.

The Messiah looked down at the young boy staring up at him and smiled.

"I'm taking you to meet my Father," he answered, "but first I must go to Jerusalem."

"Why?" the little tike asked.

"We are all getting our bodies back."

# The Over world

Joseph shook his head. "I don't understand," he admitted.

Nicodemus smiled kindly at his friend visiting from Arimathea. "I was just as confused as you," he admitted. "And then I met Joash.

"It's the fulfillment of prophecy," Nicodemus continued. "And the times are lining up perfectly. My friend, on what day did Jesus die?"

"Right before Passover. You know that, Nicodemus! We took his body from the cross! Because of that, we are unclean and not allowed to celebrate with our families."

"Yes, yes. But, don't you see, Joseph? That was the day of preparation. The day the Passover lamb is slain. A lamb without fault of blemish. His blood is put on the doorpost to protect those inside from death."

Joseph was skeptical. "And you're saying that Jesus is this lamb? His death was a sacrifice?"

"You felt the earthquake! You saw the curtain in the temple! These weren't just coincidences; they were signs! I saw and spoke to Joash. He'd come from Sheol; from Paradise. He was dead, Joseph! I went to his funeral myself!"

Joseph sighed loudly. None of this made sense. "What was it Joash had said? He was from among the First Fruits? What did he mean?"

Nicodemus nodded again. "The first of the harvest. During the Festival of First Fruits, the first fruits of the harvest are brought to the temple and presented to the High Priest as an offering."

"But the festival isn't until tomorrow," Joseph reminded him. "And Joash said that Caiaphas wasn't his High Priest."

"No, but he said he was waiting for his High Priest."

"So, who is his High Priest?"

Nicodemus grinned. "I think you know the answer to that one, my friend."

Joseph moaned. He was being dragged back into the circle again: a perpetual loop his friend was presenting that didn't make any sense. "Nicodemus," he wailed. "Jesus is dead! We buried him! You and I! He's lying in the tomb I'd purchased! It's sealed! He's not coming back!"

Nicodemus wasn't listening. He sat grinning as thoughts flashed through his mind.

"The sign of Jonah," he said. "Jesus said he would be in the earth three days and nights, like Jonah was in the whale!" Nicodemus counted them off on his fingers: "Passover, Day of Unleavened Bread, Shabbot. Three days, three sabbaths. Is it a coincidence that this year was a high sabbath with three holy days in a row? I think not! And tomorrow is the Festival of First Fruits."

He turned and looked at his friend, a smile on his face, and a gleam in his eyes.

"My friend," he said. "I don't think Jesus is going to need your tomb much longer."

# Easter Morning /
# Festival of First Fruits

"This is the one," the shepherd proclaimed, picking up the wee lamb. "He's the best one we have. Young, healthy, and not a spot on him."

"Why does it have to be the best?" his son wanted to know. "Why does it make any difference? Let's take the runty one instead. Father, the sun isn't even up yet. If we get to the temple early, it might still be too dark for the priest to look closely. No one will know."

The shepherd shook his head. "YHWH will know. And I will know. I will not try to trick YHWH. He has commanded us to bring the best of our first fruits to give as an offering: the first of our harvest. We don't have fruit, but we do have lambs. And we will do as YHWH asks.

"My son, do you not understand?" the shepherd asked. Everything we have is given to us by YHWH. Is it too much to ask that we honor him by giving him a lamb at the new year?"

"What if *I* had been born before first fruits?" the son asked with a jest. "Would you have brought *me* to the priest as a sacrifice?"

The father laughed. "Don't you remember the story of Hannah? She brought her son Samuel to the priest as a *living* sacrifice and he grew up in the temple and became our people's first prophet. But don't worry, son. We did bring a sacrifice when you were born. So yes, we gave thanks for you too."

"So," the son did some figuring in his head. "a farmer brings from his harvest. A shepherd brings from his flock. What about the blacksmith and weaver. What do they bring?"

"Money, I guess," the father shrugged. "Or perhaps the weaver would bring a bolt of cloth. It would be something to represent your trade, or money if you have a trade like a blacksmith's."

"What do the priests bring?" the son wanted to know. "They deal in souls."

The father blinked. "I...I don't know. Maybe they don't bring anything because they are the ones doing the sacrifices." He looked at his son, perplexed. He'd never really thought about it before.

The ground suddenly began shaking under their feet and the father and son struggled to keep their balance. It only lasted for a few seconds before it settled. The two stared at each other.

"That's two earthquakes in four days!" the son said when he finally found his voice again. "Do you think YHWH is angry?"

The father shook his head, unsure. "Maybe someone down below is really upset," he wondered.

# The Over World

The souls from Paradise had arisen. Bodies were reassembled and connected with the souls who owned them. Heavenly bodies. Ones that would never grow old or decay. The souls were all waiting for Jesus at the gates of heaven now, ready to be escorted into the throne room of God. Joash and the others were among them, having fulfilled their duty of telling what the Messiah had done for them. They were all waiting for Him, but Jesus was not ready yet.

He was waiting also.

The earth had shaken again when He exited the underworld and stepped into the tomb. An angel had been there to greet him as He arrayed himself once more in his body and then the angel hurled the stone away from the tomb's entrance. The event had caused all the guards to faint with fright. The entranced cleared, the angel turned, waiting for Jesus to exit before him. But the Lord looked down. The napkin that had covered his face had fallen to the floor. Jesus picked it up, folded it, and set it on the slab beside his empty burial robes. He was then ready to leave.

Jesus now stood not far from where his body had been entombed, waiting in the shadows as the sun began to rise. The angel, still at the tomb, was waiting also.

"Who can we get to roll the stone away?" they heard a voice saying. A group of women were coming down the path.

"I don't know. Maybe if we pay one of the guards will do it for us?"

"But the tomb is sealed," someone else objected. "They'd have to break the seal and that would be the death penalty."

"But..." The woman had just turned the corner and came to an abrupt halt. The tomb was open, the stone rolled away, and an angel was sitting on it.

"I know who you're looking for," he told them. "But he isn't here. He told you he wouldn't be. He's risen. Come and see. The tomb is empty. Let his disciples know what you saw and tell them he will meet them in Galilee."

Hesitantly, the women came forward, bent to look into the cave, and then ran off. Except for one. She looked in and turned to ask the angel a question. But the angel was no longer there.

Mary looked again. The tomb was definitely empty, with the burial clothes on the slab as if whoever had been in them had evaporated. Except the napkin. It was Jewish tradition to cover the face with a napkin. Why was it now folded? She'd seen similar folded napkins at dinner tables when a guest gets up to leave. A folded napkin meant they were returning and a wadded-up one meant they were done.

But this wasn't a dinner table. It was a tomb, and Jesus was gone. She'd seen him stripped and beaten, hung on a cross and breathe his last breath. One couldn't come back from that.

Overwhelmed, Mary fell to her knees and began weeping.

Jesus stepped out of the shadows and came up behind his friend.

"Why are you crying?" he asked.

She turned to look at him, but his face was still in shadow as the sun rose behind him.

"They've taken Jesus away!" She explained. "Please sir, do you know where they put his body?"

Jesus chuckled. "Mary!"

At the sound of his voice saying her name, Mary suddenly realized who was speaking. She stared at him bewildered. There were no scars on his face. His beard, which had been torn out by the angry mob had grown back. His nakedness was now covered in a robe of dazzling white.

"My LORD!" she breathed, jumping up to embrace him, but he held up a hand.

"Don't touch me!" he cautioned. "It's First Fruits. I am going up to my Father to present an offering. Today, the first of my followers are going to see God face to face.

"But now, Mary, go find the other disciples and tell them I will see them soon, and yes, Mary. We will meet again, too."

"Oh, it really is you! It's you!" Tears of joy flowed down Mary's face. "You are the Christ and Messiah!"

She turned on her heels and started running back towards town. She stopped for a moment and looked back. Jesus and the angel had vanished. She felt sad for a moment, then realized it didn't matter. He was alive and promised he'd see her again.

She started running, her feet fairly flying up the path as she shouted for all to hear. "He's alive, he's alive! I've seen him! Jesus is alive!"

# Into God's Presence

Jesus stood his back to the gates of heaven, looking over the massive crowd before him. Millions waited there in anticipation. Michael and Gabriel, the archangels helped him with his priestly robes, handing him the breastplate, belt and turban of his royal priesthood. Joash felt tears of joy and pride in his eyes as he beamed up at his high priest. In moments, all was ready, and Jesus smiled at the crowd, knowing and loving every person there.

"It is time," he announced. Michael and Gabriel pushed open the gates. The crowd, the first fruits of a new era, step through the threshold to meet their God and Father.

# Years Later

# The Underworld

Lucifer, Death, and the bookkeeper stared down at the Aggregate Scroll. Second by second, hour by hour black marks had faded to grey or disappeared altogether. Not all, but a notable percentage.

"The bridge is gone," Death grumbled. "The wall to paradise hasn't opened since *He* left. And the clean souls aren't sent here anymore. They go straight upstairs now."

Lucifer sighed loudly. "We know," he growled.

"No more contracts for the Paradise souls," the bookkeeper moaned. "*He's* taken over that too."

"Well, I got Caiaphas to pay off the guards anyway," Lucifer offered, as some solace. "Otherwise, the news about *Him* would have spread more than it has."

Death snorted. "A lot of good that did! Word got out plenty anyway!" He angrily waved a hand over the scroll, indicating all the marks that were now missing. "And setting Nero on them really helped," he added sarcastically. "All it did was spread this 'disease' out of Israel and into Africa and Europe! Hundreds of people are changing sides every minute! And that Saul of Tarsus I warned you about: he's one of the worst parasites out there!"

"It will die down," Lucifer assured him. "We've already killed off most those disciples. The only one left is imprisoned on a remote island."

"Did you see what he wrote?" Death snarled. "It's a prophecy! About YOU! Those Christian are copying it off as fast as they can get their hands on it and sending it to others! There's hundreds of Copies now, maybe thousands!" He glared hotly at the other dark lord. "You're going to lose, Lu."

"From what I read of it," Lucifer shot back, "so will you!"

"So, what are you going to do about it?"

Lucifer didn't say anything. He stared at the scroll as it slowly continued to unravel, minute by minute, to show the latest numbers of sin. They could see back into the past as far as creation, but the scroll would only allow them to unroll to the present time and no farther. It was a huge scroll. Perhaps infinitely so. At what point would their time be up? Lucifer had no way of knowing. They would have to be ready for it to be anytime.

"When we go," he finally said, "we are going to take as many of these souls with us as possible. He wants to be their Christ? Well, we are going to give them an anti-Christ. And not just one: one for every generation. We don't know when he's coming back, but I know we're going to be ready. And we won't go quietly. We are going to turn as many of these souls against him as we possibly can. By the time we're done, there won't be a person on the planet who knows who this Jesus is, let alone one who follows him. Yes, he may have won this battle, but we're going to win the war."

Death looked at his fellow Dark Lord.

*Lu,* he thought, *why do I feel this isn't going to end well?*

## Author's Note

Thank you so much for reading my short story *Three Days in Hell*. I'd always been curious as to what happened during those days Jesus was in the tomb, but it wasn't until I read the apocrypha text *The Book of Nicodemus* that I actually thought about writing a story about it. What you're holding is the results. This piece is a work of Speculative Fiction, but it is also based on biblical fact and scripture and has been proof-read by fellow Christians and theologians for accuracy.

My hope is that this story will provide you with some insight into Jewish festivals, and a more accurate concept of the "3 days and 3 nights" our savior spend in the world of the dead. There is no proof the conversations depicted actually took place, and no where in scripture will you find reference to the Aggregate Scroll or "the bookkeeper". These were purely invented for this story.

Here is your "take-away" from this tale:

We are all sinners. None of us have lived a sinless life. Because of that, our souls all bare the marks and stains of that sin.

God is sinless and pure righteousness. Sin cannot enter his presence. Because of that, we have no hope of ever being right with God and are eternally barred from his presence.

Jesus in God incarnate (God in the flesh). He willingly came to earth and lived a sinless life with the sole intent of giving up his life as payment for the sin debt that everyone else has accrued. Jesus took the sins of the world upon himself. His death paid the price for everyone, but it's only good if you accept it. That means, accepting that he lived, died, and rose again, and committing your life to following him.

There are only 2 options: living for Christ Jesus or dying in sin.

Time is getting short. Where do you want to be when it runs out?

Made in the USA
Columbia, SC
08 April 2024

34126845R00046